I'M MY OWN DOG

David Ezra Stein

CANDLEWICK PRESS

I'm my own dog.
Nobody owns me.
I own myself.

I work like a dog all day.

When I get home, I fetch my own slippers.

I curl up at my own feet.

Sometimes, if I'm not comfortable,
I tell myself to roll over.

And I do.

If someone told me, "Sit!"
I wouldn't do it.

Even if they said, "I'll give
you a bone."

Sometimes I throw a stick.

Then I go get it.

It's fun.

Every morning when I look
in the mirror, I lick my own
face because I am so happy
to see me.

I say, "GOOD DOG.
I AM A GOOD DOG."

Then I give myself a good scratch.

But there's this one spot I can't reach,

right in the middle of my back.

One time it got so bad, I let someone scratch it.

The little guy followed me home.
I felt sorry for him.

So I got a leash. How else am I supposed to lead him around?

"COME ON!" I say. "COME ON, BOY! I'LL TAKE YOU TO THE PARK."

I like showing him things.
"LOOK, LOOK, LOOK!
THAT IS A SQUIRREL," I say.

I taught him the stick game.
I have him throw.

I don't know if he understands all my commands yet, but he's learning.

"SIT, SIT. GOOD BOY."

Some folks say they're not worth the trouble. You can't keep them from yapping.

And you always have to clean up after them.

But I've grown attached to the little fella.

Between you and me, I'm his best friend.

For Hannah, who's been her own,
right from the start

First edition 2014

Library of Congress Catalog Card Number 2013952833
ISBN 978-0-7636-6139-7

14 15 16 17 18 19 CCP 10 9 8 7 6 5 4 3 2 1

Printed in Shenzhen, Guangdong, China

This book was typeset in Paquita Pro.
The illustrations' line work was created using pen as well as a kids' marker
hacked to dispense India ink; it was then photocopied onto watercolor paper.
The painting was done in liquid watercolor, with a hint of crayon on the dog's muzzle.

Candlewick Press
99 Dover Street
Somerville, Massachusetts 02144

visit us at www.candlewick.com